HALLOWEEN NIGHT

by ARDEN DRUCE   *illustrated by* DAVID T. WENZEL

rising moon

ON HALLOWEEN NIGHT,
when it's dark and scary,
who can swoop through the air
with a swish and a flurry?

"I CAN," SAID THE WITCH.

In a haunted house,
surrounded by mist,
who can spin
shimmering webs with
a swirl and a twist?

On a darkened porch,
when the moon is low,
who can light a smile
with a shine and a glow?

"I CAN,"
SAID THE
JACK-O-LANTERN.

With an eerie light,
and a shape like a lump,
who can walk
through closed doors
with a thud and a thump?

"I CAN,"
SAID THE
GHOST.

In a field of corn,
when breezes mutter,
who can stir in the wind
with a flap and a flutter?

In a twisted tree,
that's drenched in dew,
who can glide from a branch
with a hoot and a whoo?

"I CAN,"
SAID THE
OWL.

With a skull and some bones,
and no other matter,
who can dance in the wind
with a clink and a clatter?

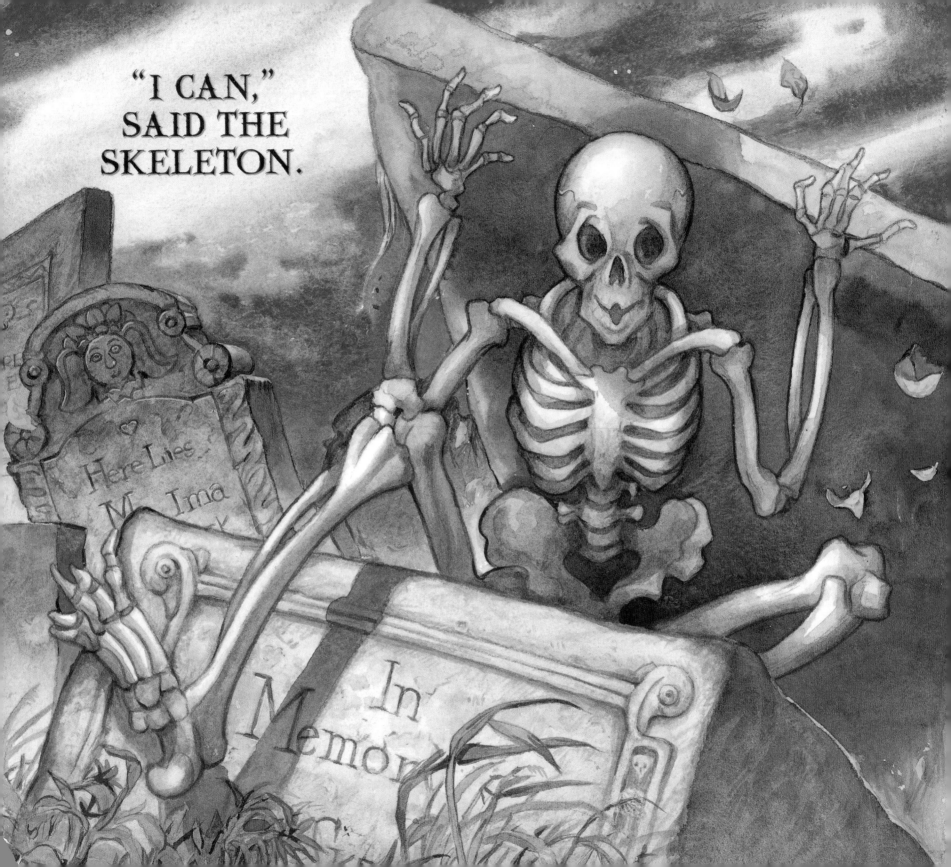

Hanging upside down,
in a tree while napping,
who can soar through the air
by fluttering and flapping?

"I CAN,"
SAID THE
BAT.

Hunched on a fence,
howling sounds you can't miss,
who can wake everyone
with a screech and a hiss?

All in their costumes,
ready for fun,
who can frighten
everyone?

ARDEN DRUCE was a school librarian and teacher for twenty-one years. She has written many classroom instructional guides for all grades, as well as several picture books including *Witch, Witch Come to My Party*, another Halloween story. Ms. Druce currently devotes her time to writing, studying, and animal welfare. She lives in Camp Verde, Arizona, with her three dogs and seven cats.

DAVID T. WENZEL is a Connecticut artist who lives with his wife and two sons on a country hillside overlooking an ancient cemetery. The rows of tilting, crumbling gravestones became the inspiration for his illustrations in *Halloween Night*. Among his best received works are illustrations for J. R. R. Tolkien's *The Hobbit*, and the adventures of the befuddled, evil wizard Bafflerog Rumplewhisker in, *The Wizards Tale*.